TRANSGRESSION OF KINSMAN

THE DELUSION

SUMEET KUMAR

Copyright © Sumeet Kumar
All Rights Reserved.

Contents

I

WAR IN THE ABYSS

In general, a lot of times it doesn't, so they're just as bad as they sure are as we log ours. Sometimes she is one, yet somewhere she never forgets her innocent friends, the evidence I am going to reveal in my alpha, maybe her importance was nothing special, yet in the world, she never lost her feet. In a way scientists are scientists in the scientific world and scientists are unusual and scientific scientists are scientists and are useful for future prediction of happiness which are like friendship. We are all kinds of dangerous alike wrong like variety creep, it's humsafar like it happens because of the silence of the gathering. Well there is going to be noise pollution when you say, we are those people in December, this type of probation again is like toh ehhi which is like silence, rhyming of minne by the words of your choice to do and made there is really only one in the world so we are gonna live here. May be wrong may be wrong: may be wrong, that too may change. Once the feathers of the aircraft are a testimony to this, it will also be a dangerous story again and again. Silence is tord of every witness. So too secure to be secure enough to be secure enough, then it's a problem of spoilage like Hug. As for the gift of the empty, the tradition of the pen is strong. Man feels the tradition of the path everyday in his gathering, no matter how much life is left, if the human heart does not change about anyone, then it is only wealth because the tradition of the society was crazy even yesterday behind the wealth and It can be dangerous only because of spoilage. ... everyone . , And then myself will not be misunderstood, will never be wrong Enemy's enemy has been identified with love and love's die, that too with true specialty God then stick with every enemy in silence, with no one in silence and no one else, then we If it is wrong, if it is wrong, then it is on its own way, lyco pyre expanded the tradition of defeating himself, say these conversation once, the world of the world has nurtured, so someone else has to be your soulmate in the unfinished journey. In the case of the world will change into the world... This is not right, therefore it is not right. Along with the use, it is also suitable to be correct and suitable for the feelings and it is doing the same thing as the feeling of feelings, sir, because if death is dead in the caste on the same day then it is fine. It is the day when our thoughts meet the feelings of trust. There is nothing in the world, if you see it, say that they are the candles of oxygen, these men are still alive, yet they keep us alive. It happens that after life, their connections are lost, our world is such a society where people only know how to survive and there are many troubles in the process of children and there are such troubles which have no solution at all. In getting the happiness of the world. In life, we are aware of all those moments which can give us pain, yet we make many unsuccessful attempts to make ourselves safe in their shadow and in the end all of them feel like a new pain. If you are lucky, then why stay with those relationships who give you two moments of happiness, their silence every moment makes us even more deprived. It is true that a person can run away from his lonely feet, he can never run away from his coming time because neither he is used to it nor any affection is with anyone in a journey, then every destination of the world feels right near the feet. In reality, even their dreams can prove to be fatal for us at times, because of this, we live very far away, you can take a break from every witness in the world. Neither will you ever let you live happily nor will you ever die Know about it in my stories, even though there is no feeling, feet are a fact that teaches me not to stop but to move forward in its place, but forgetting every accident, I am happy only to move ahead and if Even when happy moments are visible in front, I stay away from them because the destination never stops at one place, this enough keeps going on like the wind. foot the whole world is up.

"I have seen heartbreak
and breaking myself also
but besides this , i want to hug her
becuase her cheating gives me a another turn
of facing the mirror also."

This is the last gift, which I am going to write, that too about my beloved gathering, from which I can never be afraid, nor can I tell God to keep it away, I am so much known that I have been ruined. Probably every time I recommend to be ruined: I am not giving respect I used to keep myself safe in my heart, even though it is a small and true show of my journey, there are some paths in it too, which pass only because of the pain.

"Everyone have left me
for whom i have to request now.
there are some place of silence in my part
which is left now.
so , the time has come to go back to home now."

II
THE UPPER CLASS OF GRAVEYARD

Whatever I am about to say today, his silence may not
be liked by every witness, yet I can never end my talk about

something because what I eat with deceit is probably not small, life is for everyone to learn and learn. For me, my life does not give me a second chance, neither that second chance nor its second word ever took birth, yet I always say that I should never give up my efforts, go closer to the bash and feel my loneliness and Walk myself close to him like a companion, it was probably not possible because the way in which his shadow was on my feet was the reason for my ruin, every time enough used to request him to forget everything and try to move forward Feet was it possible, I never even knew that feet are saying that the distance we have taken in the depths of both of us will ever be able to change, this is not a love story, feet are a story, it is a story and a story whose strength is there. had given us both a shishkdar toad that the desire to connect had died, as the world is full of things, just like nowadays people also become artificial. And their baatis, yards and emotions, everything has become bash banabati, the world has become a bad thing about the wrong thing, in the love one should get the words and feelings of the other and not the smell of the body and wealth should be found in the feet is it right what is right in me happy day undefined The relationship I have with someone was right No, his only memories are those in which he has neither included me nor has given any partner. So let's make famous those friends, in whom till date could not forget their words, I had tried a lot to forget myself and I had tried to the extent that I was looking for their happiness even after being deprived, that too in a place where my loved ones The way of my grave was decided. So this is my story, maybe nothing special, feet is a way to cover a journey, maybe show a lot of paths, why every time the gathering is never the same and every day show the same saying, this too Still it is not possible, even if the true reason for the silence is not understood today, then I may be missing my part too because of myself, a witness had said a very good thing, that whatever you have lost, you have lost it because of yourself. lost no one else is the reason for your silence only you can finish what you started in the beginning and this philosophy has become the definition of my life which means to move forward as well as move after me so when did these accidents happen undefined undefined how it happened Well, whatever it is, all of you will get the news, before that all of you should be aware of my words and my character, because even though the hero of the story is someone else, the story of my existence is also found to a great extent. In Rajveer Khurana, a boy who never did any work in his entire life, yet the boundary of my ego remained at the top and that's because my father who was behind me means that in his house he was an unworthy child whom two witnesses He had taken care of it in a very good way and that too because both of them used to love, they knew that my love could never change and they didn't have any problem with me, I mean to say that they liked my lifestyle. Parvar Singh had some respect that I used to explain myself as a Nawab and why not understand that whatever I aspired to become the dust of my feet, it used to go with me, that every relationship in the world can be cheated and this So it has become quite common nowadays that the feet in whose feet there is an arc of heaven, neither are those relationships above even God's soul and in what way? I am doing things not only of my mother and father but of my mother and father. Normally people consider their parents as their whole world, feet for me they are not only my world but my stability, if I say chemikallya then for me they are my balancing I have power, I can never separate from him and he can never separate himself from me likewise my dad is a business vaccine by profession and my mother is a lawyer, dad's recipe he made his own feet my family my dad It is because of my mother and it is because of my mother. According to his luck, I had the last fault for my mother and father, if I say in normal language, then such a fate that no one used to say to make my own. It means that it is incomplete in the right foot, I tell my mother and father. I didn't have blood, meaning when I was born, I was born with an orphan, meaning my own parents left me because I did it because they think that I am abnormal, that means my body language is abnormal because the tragedy of my life was such that the doctor had separated my mother and father from my entry foot, now because of this accident to you all Let me make you aware, then the accidents were such that when I entered the world of God, then my feet were abnormal, which means that the doctor had a wish that I could never say, that's why he had left me in a happy hosipta, that too would give birth. I don't know how much truth is behind the mystery even though I may have written it because at that time I knew that my real parents were dead. Anshuman Khurana and Arpita Singh Khurana, how do I know this thing: There are many secrets behind who told this, which may be revealed in time. There was only a drain in everyone's eyes, if I say in tapori language, because in my small right world Hyderabad was then meaning my mother and father's birth place was Hyderabad. The one who hasn't even seen his real parents, how about his hometown: How will he get a child? Well society's lights never hurt me He was not my real mother and father, yet I loved him even more than my real mother and father and both of them used to love me more than his real son, he never let me feel the silence of the thing that I I do not have my own blood, in the same way I have not mixed all of you with my elder brother. I mean my big bodyguard then who was the big hulk of our small right world and there is a secret behind why he became hulk undefined Well I will definitely tell his words because his life is always comedy I mean to say since childhood But till today there was no serious thing in his life, so the matter is such that when my brother used to study in 10th standard, he fell in love with the daughter of a wrestler and that too means that girl does not love him then what was that? He was running in a race where his ancestry was not confirmed, he had to face action tragedy in the affair of love tragedy. I am a date with respect and I do a little work related to his pain, instead of increasing, I did not even tell my brother's pain because in those days his name was screwed, Kabir Khurana, who had no troubles in his entire school because father's power It was something like this, that's why even the teachers never used to give any punishment to them because they The school was ours, they also used to make a lot of mistakes because of fearlessness and later they used to sleep all day after listening to their father's scolding. There is a son and there is a boy and now there is also a child, it becomes a mistake and if the child will not do it in age, then when will it? ? Feet in a mother's court, her son is never guilty, say that she should not commit a crime, because that mother understands everything that we cannot do with anyone else, where father's arguments used to end, that mother's court It used to start and I have already expressed that my mother was a lawyer and because of her conversation, many judges had signed their transfer order feet and hit the arc of permanent approval on them, so how long will my father's arguments work? In the coming and going thing, he never used to do anything and even if he did, my brother would have protected me at that time, which is the story of every household these days. I never ask my words and even if by mistake he goes to the pouch, he never says anything to me, I remember some of his words in bash exception, which was in some way that Satyadas Mahto is undefined If you make any mistake again then your big Like a brother, you will also be punished, understand undefined Papa, whenever I speak these batis, I see only the value of the question mark in the definition of my retarded because I hear his conversation one ear and the other one's feet would come out of his conversation heart. Wasn't upset hot because I knew that he had love for me too Only humanity was not shown because only human beings can show humanity, not gardeners and I was strict not to dress with those human Gods because only God can make a mistake once. I am saying in part, in reality, that their destiny is even higher than this, my family Every witness in the war was aware that I am not his own blood, I am not his son, even Kabir Brother knew this very well, yet he never made him realize that I am not his own brother, whenever I Some would say that he would have given me a bash whenever something was done, it would have been present even before I could think of it. Well before my words will keep going, let me complete Kabir Brother love story before that which was incomplete. So on the morning of the accident, it was such that Kabir Bhai used to love a girl, that too in our school time, who was the daughter of wrestlers and the name of the girl was Said Deepti Gujjar, who is very beautiful feet dangerous even they say not of the world. Every beautiful thing is dangerous, even if it is unsurpassed, and to get it, we need courage, not determination, and Kabir Brother had gone a little weak at the time, I have already told that Kabir Bhai was from him. They used to love one side, that means they were in love on the other side, because Deepti Gujjar never got a chance to see anyone else because her marriage was decided by her parents and uncle in her childhood. Had given and I never had the news of the conversation to Kabir Brother, it means that if there were conversation between them, then perhaps it would have been recommended to open the secret, the feet would have been undefined whenever the brilliance came to school, their two wrestlers would have stayed together. Who was none other than his own rule runs and no one in the whole school had the courage to wander beside him because whoever had made this mistake before this, his hands and feet were not left, that means his goons toad his hands and feet. They were given in front of the whole school, these conversation are from long ago and I too have only heard many words and have never seen them. That's why Kabir Brother never spoke to him because he was well aware of the teachings that If he ever made any mistake then mother would be very hurt and father would throw him out of the house because he was some common man. The girl was not there and even if there was a good time between the two, then they would never have been married and their age was not very special at the time that they should do all this, still they were in love, so this thing is bound to wait for a lover I mean that we can never wait and how many of us stayed in his prison, after all one day the curtains were about to rise, feet before it is too late Let us also see what did Kabir Bhai do that even his father stopped supporting him. So this thing would probably be on 14th June when Kabir Brother had shown the words of love for Deepti Gujjar. He was noticing them for a long time, he never looked back at Kabir Brother, nor did he ever ask him to share, yet Kabir Brother did not give up every effort because love would have been such that even the thirsty would get the sea. This thing is only to be said, how much truth is there in this, even I do not know, then did Kabir Brother think that on this day, why should nothing happen today? I will keep telling him the things of my heart, say why his wrestler should not beat me, he says when someone has a new love, nor I mean to say first love, then he can do anything for his pen at that time. And this is mostly done by the boy because our Amitabh Bachchan sir has said in his pronunciation that men never feel pain, in reality they were so much sticks beyond that they had seen Charminar, well what happened after all.

CONVERSATION

"

Kabir : deepti ! what can i told you?
Deepti : if someone will see you we will be in trouble ! Go away, what do you have to say here, you go away.

Kabir : No, I will just keep saying my words.
Deepti : If my uncle sees then you will not be able to say that, he sees that he is also coming!
Kabir : Let it come, whatever happens today, I will see, the foot that is going on inside me can bear no more, I don't have the courage at all.
Deepti : Say it well, if anything bad happened to you, then call me a wheeze, understand it.

__Kabir__ : Ok.
*__Deepti__ : Now tell me quickly, what do you want
to say?"*

Before this, Gujjar wrestlers saw both of them talking, even before their conversation continued to grow, then what was Kabir brother then that day of time in a pure warm blooded to share the feeling in the front of deepti ,that I love you, tell you to marry, tell you to make my own, for a long time. I love you now, understand my condition and my condition, I have fallen in love with you, when I have seen you Uncle's wrestlers used to always stay with you, so I could never say my feet, today I will say that no matter what happens. Before that, he would say something in front of it, a slap from there and after that the wrestlers of "after washing" Deepti Gujjar Gave them in the form of a gift, then what was our light brother's ground foot and his love for heaven's foot, I really understood in the day that in love the earth and the sky look alike: why look and why are alike. What was it then? In the whole school, it started going that there should be a fight between the wrestlers of Kabir Khurana and Deepti Gujjar. It's gone, and this thing was a little bit hidden by dad, because even though dad used to work, now it was his son's thing and his son whom he considered too unworthy of me, when dad came to know about this, then he Was not with him in time, means I was with my mother, she was also out for some work and when we came to know that Kabir brother is very young and he has been beaten by Gujjar wrestlers, then mother and I immediately came from him and dad then it was present before his feet, he did nothing for Kabir Brother at that time, on the contrary, he threw his own son out of his own school, neither did he listen to his brother nor saw him, as soon as he came, he Gujjar A complaint was made against the family and that too under the act of half murder, then what was the mother, she was already a lawyer, she could not see the pain of others, so she had come to her own son's feet, so she How would he have left him when the mother filed a case against him, then the father took it back because he thought that his son had made a mistake, so why would he file any other leg several times? Do. After that, only their donation fulfills our dream, if you want to leave the endowment of the destination, then leave it completely, then even God shows us the unfulfilled dream, the beginning of fulfilling it is only in our hands and the time is mine. The destination was like this, it could have lost itself in time, it could have deprived itself of itself was , I could never break their trust .

"You are a small smile on a face
but i am the whole mirror of yours
but i have go through the many steps more
than the dreams we have seen
i don' t know the value of the world , so i have
attached in the relationship of yours
by always calling brother brother
i have been lived in the strong arms of yours."

"More than my family , outsiders have handled
me
hoping about the dark , they cradle me with
the light.
for what i have to do arguments
for mistakes , they have called me my lovely
son with more shine as a light."

In life, it is not necessary that it is really your own, because of the passion of blood, relationships are never formed, the eyes are also really necessary, to ride it, water, air and many things are needed to make a plant a tree. trust is also very much needed to improve a person like happiness, whose education is neither available in the market nor can we ever buy it. That I have not yet seen the whole truth nor can I show it because my defeat is present in their defeat, which I cannot accept by saying that it is necessary, yet I cannot get them because even when there are some pains like this, we will never have any other health , never can share.

III

FELONY OUT OF THE SIGHT

The education of crime is also such that she never sees
the relationship and says that she is of blood, why
unknowingly, her thinking would have been for everyone
and the person who committed the crime to your

relationship, it is a different matter. If we are of blood, then it is inevitable that we can forget the pain that comes from them. Can't say no matter how hard you try, the share of crime is not right for everyone because it is also a better understanding of relationships and wealth than us and it is so cruel that when someone's love and love get out of your mind. Throw it away and after that you don't even have a small clue about it. Well there are some moors in life from whom we try to stay very far, yet neither we ever get away from them nor do we ever get away from them. You can try to forget the moments, I never thought that my life will change in such a way that I will not be able to bother myself even in the senses and only the lights There was also a few things to whom people gave the trouble of the accident, on this day something happened when they beat Kabir Brother with the wrestlers of Gujjar, on that day they physically forgot him, they were not able to forget him mentally because till today his On the other hand, no one even raised his hand and never spoke to him in a loud voice, so he could not forget those moments, enough had become devastated in himself because at that time dad had told him a lot and had misunderstood Neither did he give them a chance to speak nor tell them that a crime starts only when you are proved wrong by being right and Kabir brother was never wrong, he had only expressed his love which was In my eyes, it is not at all wrong, on the day when Kabir brother met, his condition was so bad that he could not even stand properly, in his condition he could not even see with his eyes, enough I am doing Was that those who have done this condition of them, I should not leave them alive, my suffocation was getting right, seeing their pain, I told them every problem. I used to say to hurry, so I did what I wanted to do at the time, I had thought that I would kill them if I would not leave them alive and I had also taken this place to a great extent, everything is possible in a foot bailout. He used to say that he should not be punished for this, he never thought that anything like this would happen. After all, who did it and why? Kabir brother did not do it and if he did, why did he punish me? Why am I guilty? Why am I guilty of undefined crime? Why is my share of happiness? Why are people imprisoning me in the pain of suffering and that too on my own. It must have happened the day mom was not home nor dad was there and I had just finished my classes that I saw everything scattered, seeing everything scattered, I was a little upset at the time, so I called Kabir brother at the time. There was no response and when I went to his room, he was not there, then I checked the garden area, so he was not there either. I was very scared at the time, so I called mom and dad, feet were telling their call out of out of reachable and many times when I tried to switch off, I was not even in a state to think for the time being, was feeling strange again. I searched Kabir brother in every corner of the house up and down many times, yet he could not find me, I was so scared that time I thought that I would have to call the police now, so I went inside the house to lane my phone. When I ask him, my phone was also missing, I was quite surprised at the time that what is happening in school and where my mother and father are in danger and Kabir brother, where is there any danger on them undefined I was thinking all this that then I remembered that I can also call landline undefined In spite of all this I left my house and ran straight towards the police station when I was running towards the police station. I saw mom and dad means that they were also going on the road, I saw them and sounded many times, they did not even look at me behind them, because they were going after them fast and when I asked the police station, i see mama dad is already there to see dead body of kabir brother undefined

Conversation

"**Mom** : *Where is my son??*
Police : *Till now your son's face has not been fixed identified because the one who killed your son first put acid on his face so that no one can digest his face and then many times his head was crushed with hammer.*
Mom : *What are you saying Anshuman , It can't happen that my son can't die (Emotions of Weeping).*
Dad : *Arpita just keep calam , Whatever have happened and it's not necessary that the body is of our Kabir. I was not going close to her, I was scared of bashing, thinking that my loved ones were showing tears. Seeing that I myself had become weak and when I went close to him, he asked me that we had given you such good upbringing and taught you so well, then why did you kill my son, why did you kill Kabir? Meaning what happened undefined how my life has changed so much. The mother who has never separated me from herself is accusing me of being the killer of her pride undefined I killed her son.*
Me : *Dad , What mother is saying now , I can never think to hurt my dearest brother kabir, I can't*

kill him, Dad can never think of hurting myself and I am also your beta and not dad again How can mother speak to me like this, I could not understand anything at that time, that means my life will change so much in a moment, that too for my own sake, I never thought that I cried many times in front of dad and then mother He did not listen to one of my feet in front, till this dad told me that you are not our blood, only we have brought you up and we ever thought that we are raising a snake in our house, which will be our son tomorrow. Why did we give you so much and in return you took the life of our son."

For the first time in life, even after being right, he used to say to be wrong, neither did he have the courage nor the courage to prove himself in front of him that I have not done anything like this, if someone else speaks these words, then she also Those who took my feet from the batis of my grave had said that they were ready, well everyone must be thinking that or how all this happened, the evidence must have been received by all those whose stupidity they consider me to be guilty, that too for a crime. Which I have never done nor can I ever think to do. The police wished that I did this crime because they got the murder pot foot my ring which was given to me by my mother and father when I was 5 years old. Because of a proof, he accepted me as a crime. I will strangle the person who killed my Kabir with my own hands.

"Nor he have given me the time to think
Neither he decided the date to fight

***But coincidently where i am deprived in the
memories of my family
On that place he have down me to the
graveyard in the night***"

There are also some accidents which are very different from our ordinary life, there is no cost of thinking in the world and the importance of loved ones is also a lot of work, we can talk to a stranger about our pain, our feet are never our own health and nowadays this is our world. The biggest mistake is that no one will be with you all the time, everyone knows this, yet despite being helpless, they try to get the true witness which is not worthy of our grace, not only I have seen one thing in my relationship that I have definitely noticed. I never belonged to me, they never belonged to me, they do not have their fault in their eyes in a filled gathering, I did nothing to show them because my heart was wasted inside my heart was wasted to listen to their arguments After trying to hurt herself all the time, the bailout of the accident will always remain incomplete because even my existence was killed by my own people on this day. To bring the whole truth to the fore, enough could say at the last moment that I was not wrong and neither did he bother I can give those who have brought me up, the story character is still many and many mysteries which are yet to be revealed and the recommendation to break what my enemies have prepared for me is still pending. Before leaving, tell me a few things. provide say that the dead body that the police got at the right time was not that of Kabir brother, but only me and the witness know these things, who had helped me and those people who had saved themselves in the gift of relationships. I had prepared the grave of my death. Neither the journey is incomplete nor the participants of the crime are still incomplete, the feet are some questions whose answers are still unanswered, why did they happen, when did they do it and how? There are many secrets which are yet to be revealed There are many mysteries on which the curtains are yet to be removed, then beginning will have to wait, many of these games have not been created by my own undefined and even if Kabir has died, then who did it and why undefined Many of these Gujjars Wrestler then it will be never undefined Is this really what Rajveer has killed undefined And if he hasn't killed his brother Kabir then why did he go to jail considered himself to be guilty for a crime he could never commit.

*"Incomplete but many characters of crime is still
pending
and who have think that the story have ended
with the time
but the whole war is not at the ending."*

Jazmin

EDITION : 1

www.ingramcontent.com/pod-product-compliance
Lightning Source LLC
Chambersburg PA
CBHW020856160726
47993CB00004B/1686